Mel Bay Presents

Forty Studies for Violin

by Herbert Chang

1 2 3 4 5 6 7 8 9 0

Visit us on the Web at www.melbay.com — E-mail us at email@melbay.com

Contents

NOTES ON THE STUDIES

Study No. 1: This is a study for basic bowing strokes. It should be practiced with the recommended bowings. All the chords in this study should be played unbroken.

Study No. 2: When performing shifting, move the entire hand to the new position instead of using the fingers to search for the notes. Keep the finger action simple and clean. Slide should not be noticeable.

Study No. 3: Using a four note bowing pattern to play six notes' worth of music is demonstrated in this study. It is a very fine exercise to develop a quick mind for bowing control. This piece should be practiced with the recommended bowings. Accent should be played on the beat all the time.

Study No. 4: Building up technical control in the fingers of the left hand is the aim of this study. The left hand should be relaxed and kept in a nice round shape. The fingers should remain on the fingerboard as long as possible, and the lifted fingers should stay just above the note about to be played. Again, keep the finger action simple and clean.

Study No. 5: In this study, down-bow chords are played first, then up-bow chords, and finally they are combined. You may practice this piece at the most comfortable tempo first and then gradually get into the marked tempo.

Study No. 6: The entire study should be performed on the G-string. For the purpose of practice, this piece also can be played on the D string in E minor, on the A string in B minor, and on the E string in F♯ minor.

Study No. 7: Not only is this study an excellent left-hand exercise, it is also a very fine piece for developing a clear and quick mind. For the purpose of practice, the fingers may even be lifted higher and then struck back on the fingerboard quickly.

Study No. 8: A fast détaché and a sautillé are alternately performed in this study. It requires a very high level of bowing control. Clear bowing difference should be shown every time when the bowing strokes changes.

Study No. 9: You may practice this study with a more controlled spiccato first and then gradually change the bowing strokes to the less controlled sautillé. Again, a clear bowing difference should be shown every time when the bowing strokes changes.

Study No. 10: I highly recommended this study. It offers a great opportunity for the development of flexibility and technical control in the fingers of the left hand. The fingers should remain on the fingerboard until the end of the marked underline. Care should be taken so that the left hand is not tight when the fingers are stretched hard.

Study No. 11: Bowing control for single notes, double-stops, and chords are all different. In this study, they are mixed together to provide an excellent bowing exercise. The entire study should be played with broad strokes of the bow. All the chords should be played unbroken.

Study No. 12: This extremely difficult exercise will force all the left-hand fingers to effectively build up their strength and technical control. For the purpose of practice, fingers may even be lifted higher and then struck back on the fingerboard quickly. Care should be taken so that the left hand is not tight. If tension starts to build up, stop practicing and take a break.

Study No. 13: Building up precise bowing control is the purpose of this study. The suggestion is to start practicing this piece with shorter bowing strokes first and then gradually increase bowing length and power after confidence is built up. Accent should be played on the beat all the time.

Study No. 14: Because the 1st and 3rd fingers always remain on the fingerboard, the 4th finger has to work independently in this exercise. It will force the 4th finger to quickly build up its power and technical control. The 4th finger should not be tight but under control.

Study No. 15: The trills in this study are similar to the previous exercise but short and quick. Again, the 4th finger should not be tight, and the trills should be under control.

Study No. 16: A very fast martelé bowing and a very slow singing bowing are played alternately in this study. An outstanding bowing control is needed to handle the two opposite bowings in one piece. Use the whole bow to play the entire study and do not change tempo to facilitate different bowing strokes.

Study No. 17: In this piece, all the fingers of the left hand are used sequentially to play the non-stop trills. This practice session will highlight the weak finger and force the finger to build up its strength to match the others'. The unused fingers should be kept on the fingerboard as much as possible to eliminate unnecessary finger lifting.

Study No. 18: You will need a clear mind as well as a good finger control to play this study. While practicing, a short break between each trill can be added and then taken out when the exercise is mastered. Tempo for this study is variable.

Study No. 19: From a long, slow bowing to a short, fast détaché, a variety of speeds of bowing strokes is shown in this study. It will highlight the bowing which the violinist has not yet mastered. The entire piece should be played with an even tempo. A metronome can be used to keep you from changing the tempo to facilitate different bowing strokes.

Study No. 20: This is a wonderful exercise to develop nimbleness and quickness in the fingers of the left hand. The trills should be quick and under control. The left hand should not be tight.

Study No. 21: A long, slow bowing is used to play single notes, double stops, and even chordal music in this study. It requires tremendous bowing control to handle the bowing difference between the three. All the slow chords have to be played broken, but the bass voice should be held as long as possible.

Study No. 22: This is another highly recommended exercise. It offers a great opportunity for the development of power, independence, and technical control in the fingers of the left hand. Care should be taken so that the left hand is not tight when the fingers are stretched hard. If the left hand is tired, take a break immediately.

Study No. 23: When performing this exercise, the left hand should be kept in a nice round frame, which is the best hand shape to play double stops. The left hand should be relaxed, and the unused fingers should be kept on the fingerboard as much as possible.

Study No. 24: Again, maintain a nice hand shape, particularly at the fast section. When performing note changes, move the fingers on the fingerboard instead of lifting fingers off the string.

Study No. 25: Fingered octaves require a very high level technical control in the fingers of the left hand. As only a relaxed left hand can demonstrate such control, special attention should be paid so that the left-hand fingers are always relaxed and under control.

Study No. 26: Keeping the fingers relaxed and under control is the key to master tenths. While practicing this exercise, tension should be carefully avoided. If tension starts to build up, take a break immediately.

Study No. 27: All the basic double stops, which including thirds, sixths, fingered octaves, and tenths, are shown in this study. When performing this exercise, special attention should be paid so that the left hand is not tight and the fingers are under control.

Study No. 28: The entire study should be played with the lower part of the bow. Tension should be carefully avoided when the left-hand fingers are stretched hard. If the left hand is tired, stop practicing and take a break.

Study No. 29: To develop a nice hand frame is the goal of this study. The left hand should be kept in a nice round shape all the time. The fingers should remain on the fingerboard as much as possible. Keep the finger action clean.

Study No. 30: This exercise is designed for developing a high level left-hand technique. The left hand should be relaxed, and the trills should be under control.

Study No. 31: Use the broad strokes of the bow to play the entire study. While performing string-crossing, keep the bowing horizontal changes as small as possible. The string crossing should not be noticeable.

Study No. 32: An outstanding finger independence can be achieved by practicing this study. The trills should be played strictly in time, as 32nd notes. The left hand should not be tight at all.

Study No. 33: A variety of chords are shown in this study. The entire piece should be played with a very powerful bowing attack. The accent should be played on the chords all the time even if the chords do not occur on the beat.

Study No. 34: Do not let the unusual nature of these trills scare you off. Actually, most violinists can master them. While playing this exercise, the fingers should not be tight and the trills should be under control. As long as the trills are under control, you are on the right track.

Study No. 35: The trills in this study are similar to those in the previous exercise but short and quick. Again, the fingers should not be tight and the trills should be under control.

Study No. 36: This technically difficult study can be mastered only if the left hand is not tight. The trills should be under control all the time. If tension starts to build up, stop practicing and relax the hand immediately.

Study No. 37: Again, special attention should be paid so that the left hand is not tight and the trills are under control. If the left hand is tight, stop practicing and take a break.

Study No. 38: This piece should be played like two violinists playing a duet. All the quarter notes and half notes should be performed as long as possible even though their bowing strokes cannot be that long.

Study No. 39: This is a three-voice study. It should be performed like a trio. If the bowing strokes for some notes cannot be played as long as the value marked in the score, their voice should be held as long as possible.

Study No. 40: The last piece is a four-voice bowing study. Clear bowing character should be shown for each variation. All the chords should be played unbroken except the last one. Again, if the bowing strokes for some notes can not be played as long as the value marked in the score, their voice should be held as long as possible.

Herbert Chang

40 STUDIES

1.

Herbert Chang

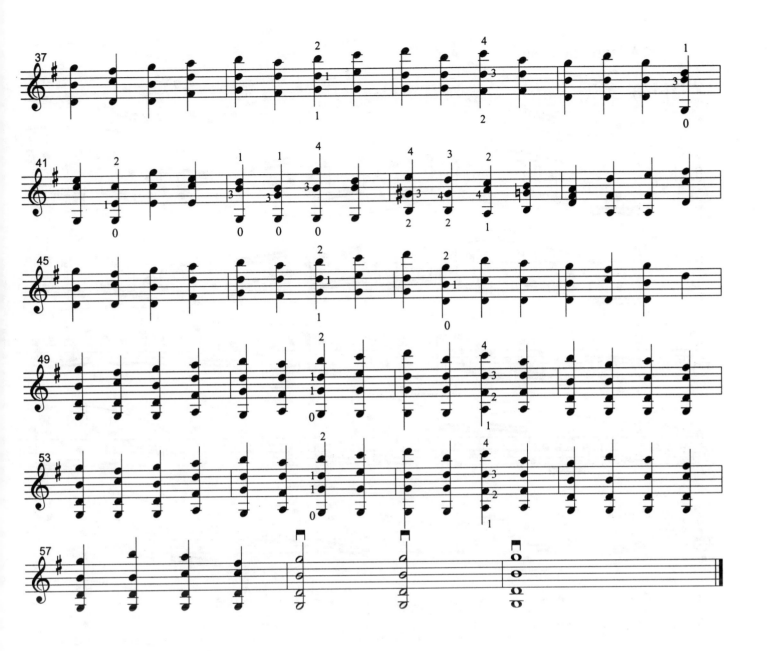

Bowings for Study No.1

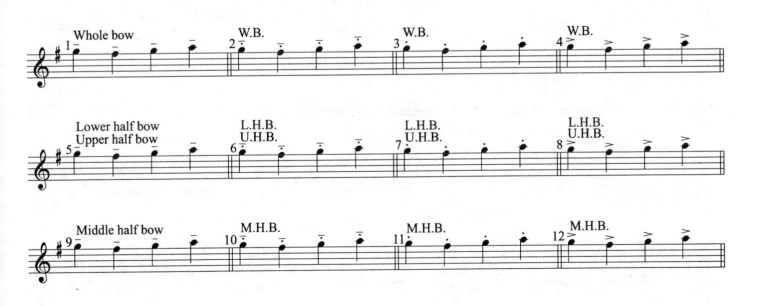

2.

9

3.

Bowings for study No. 3

11

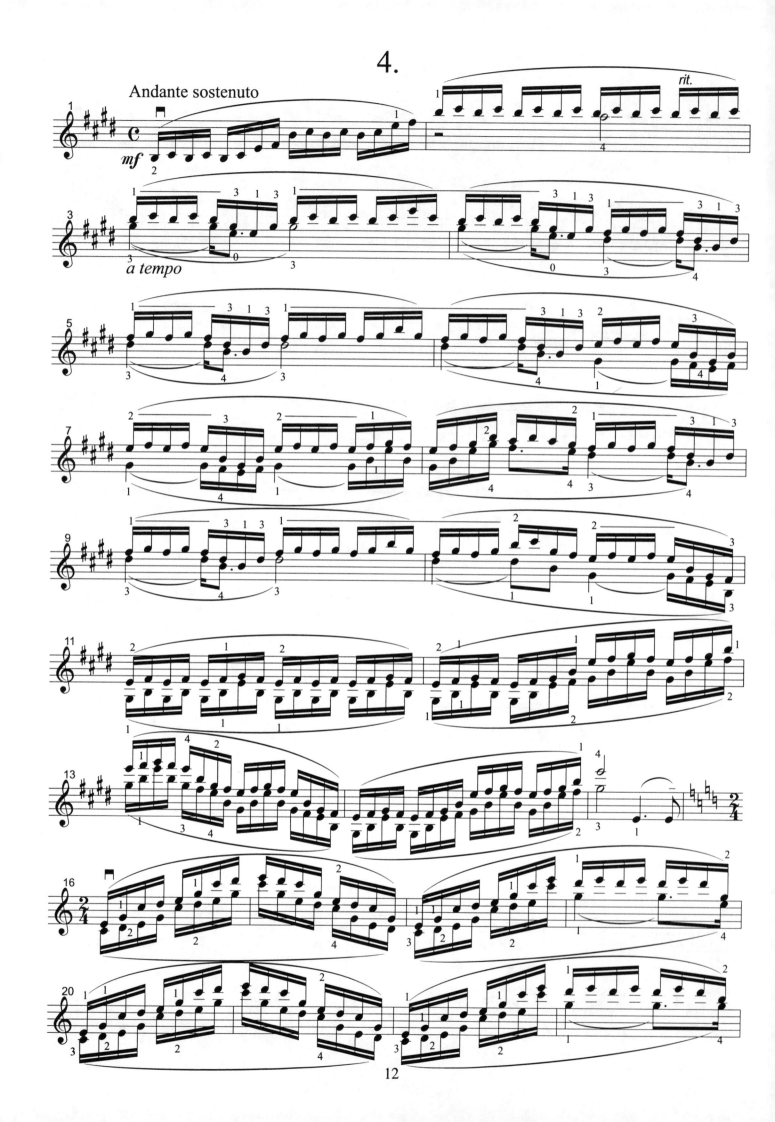

4.

Andante sostenuto

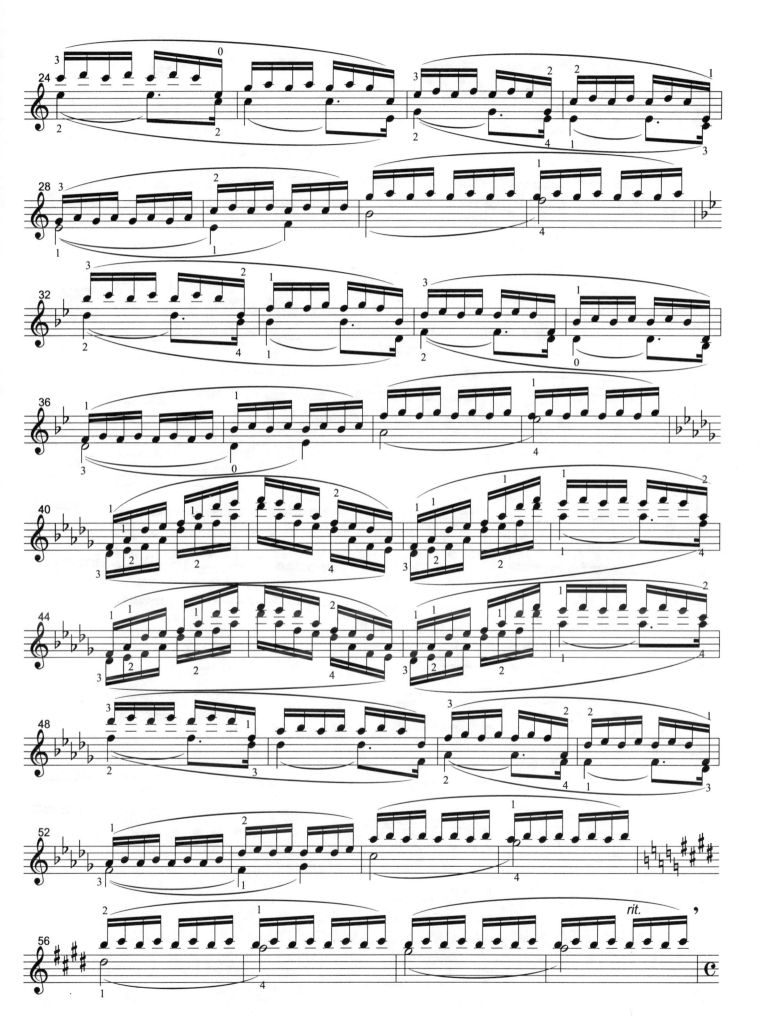

13

14

5.

Moderato

6.

7.

Rhythms for study No. 7

8.

21

9.

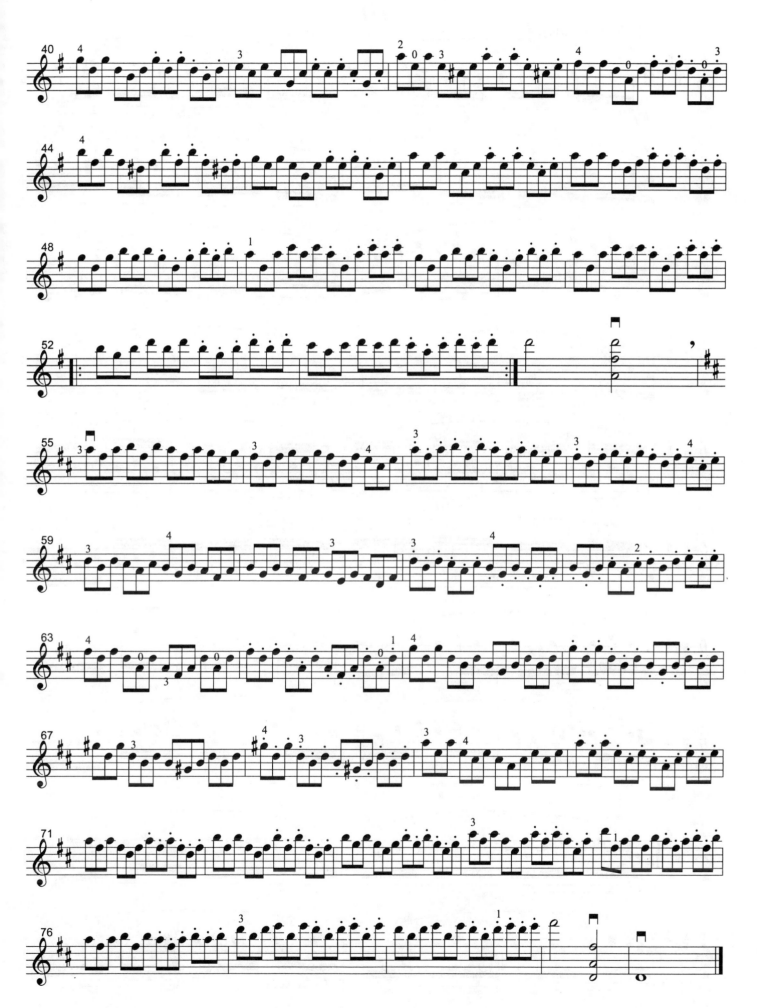

10.

11.

12.

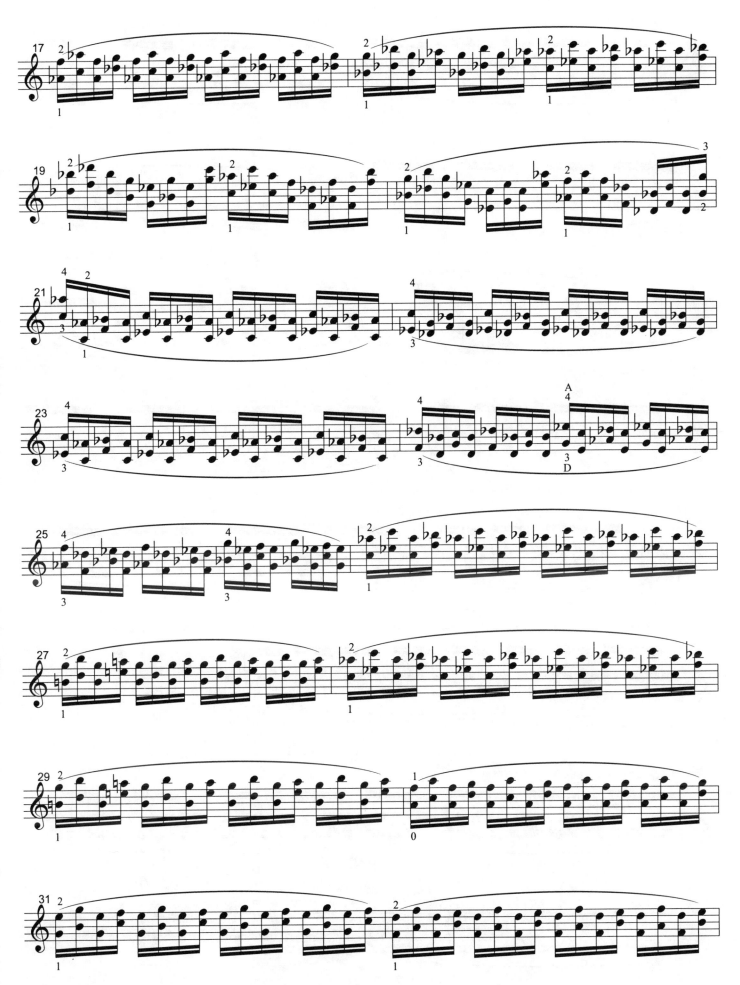

Rhythms for Study No. 12

13.

15.

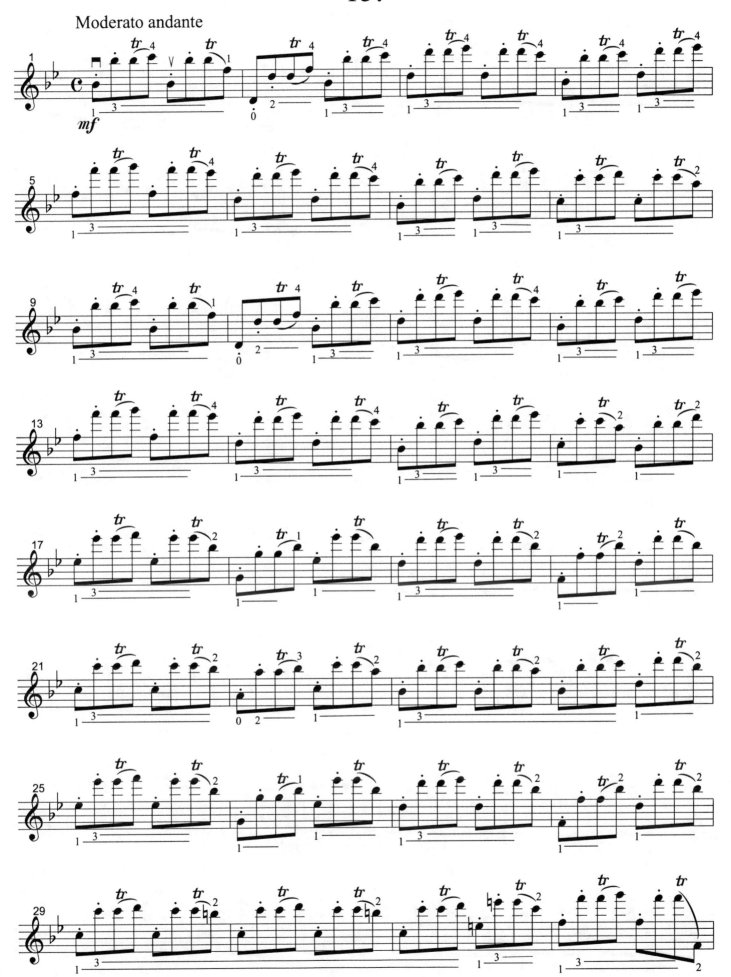

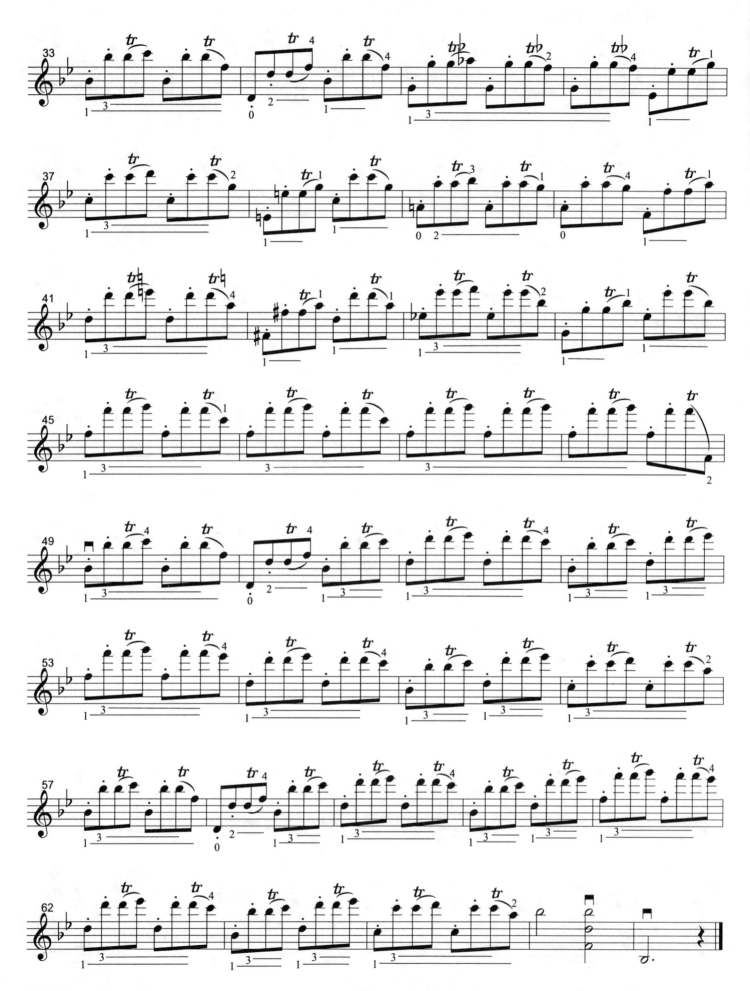

34

35

18.

19.

20.

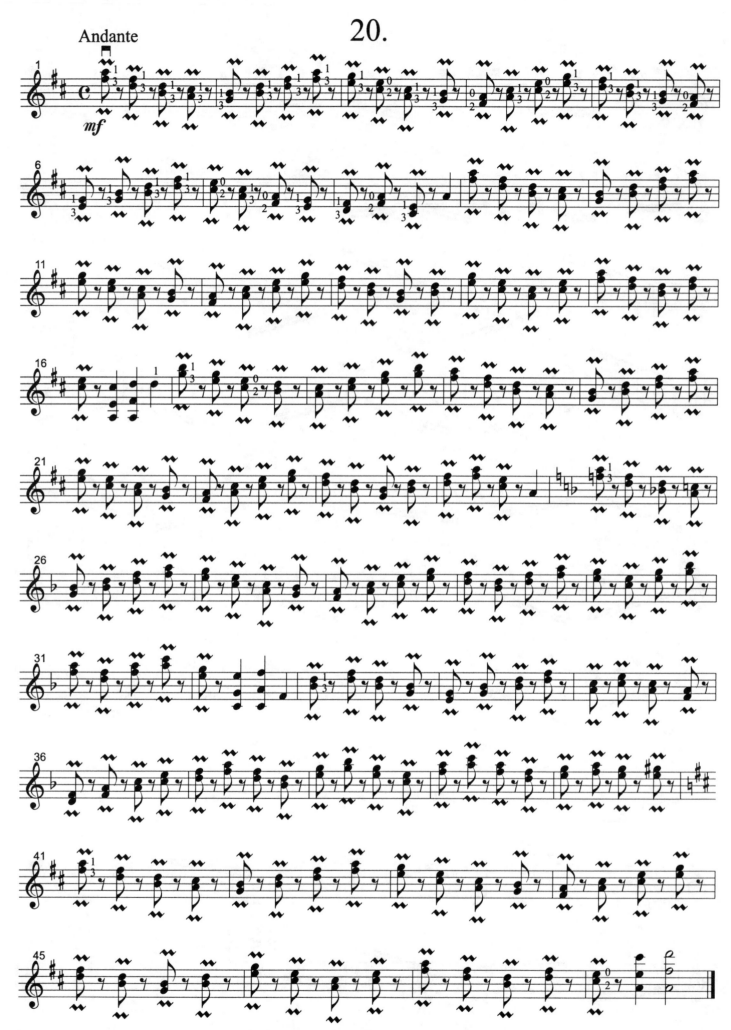

21.

Moderato andante

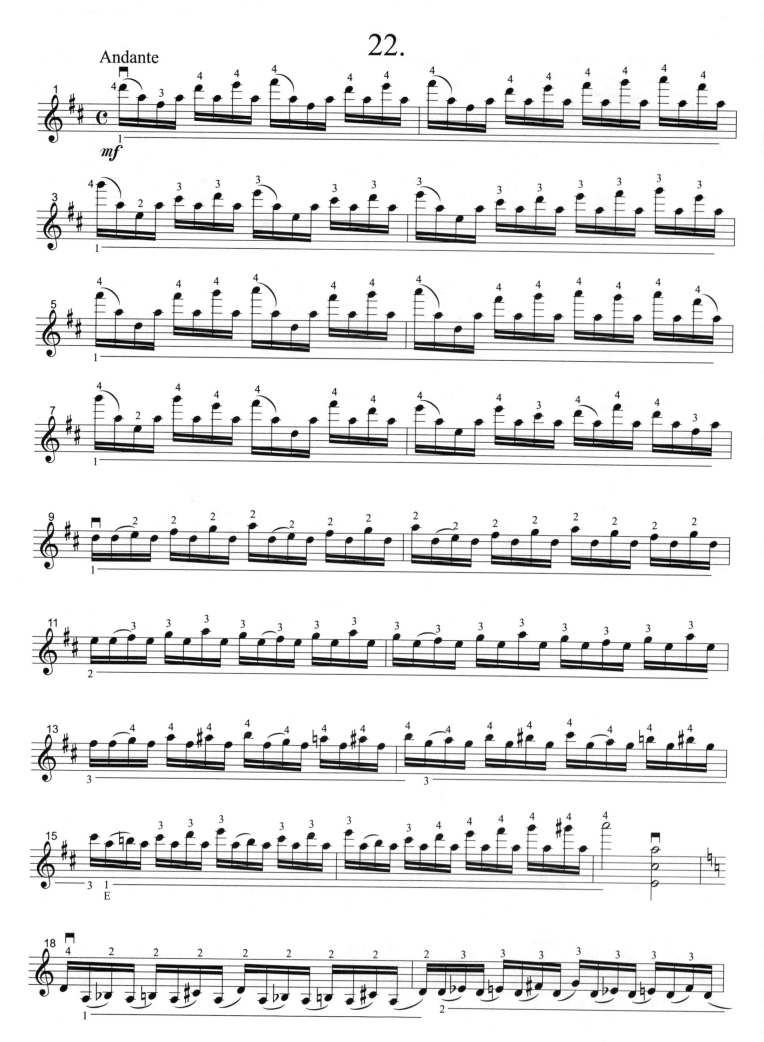

23.

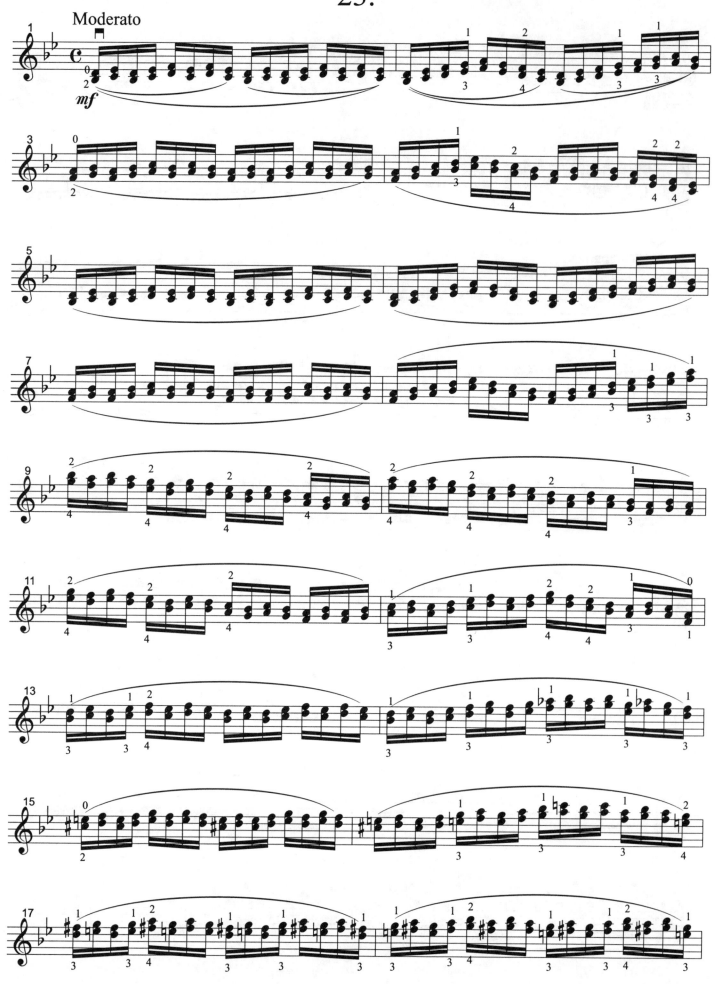

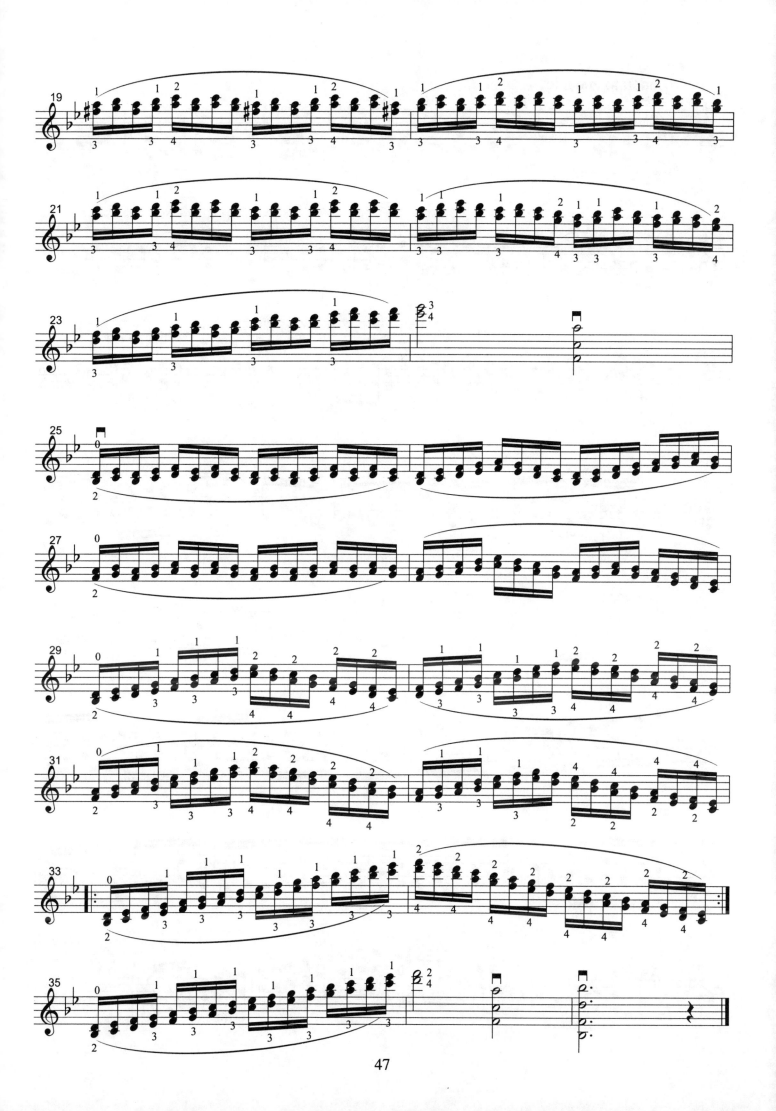

24.

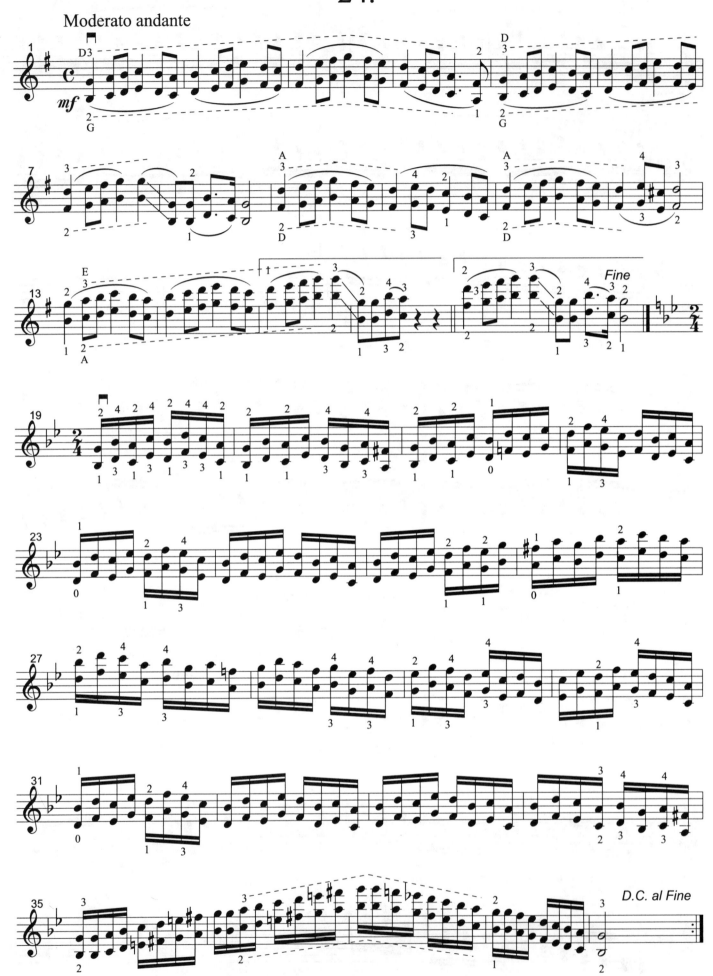

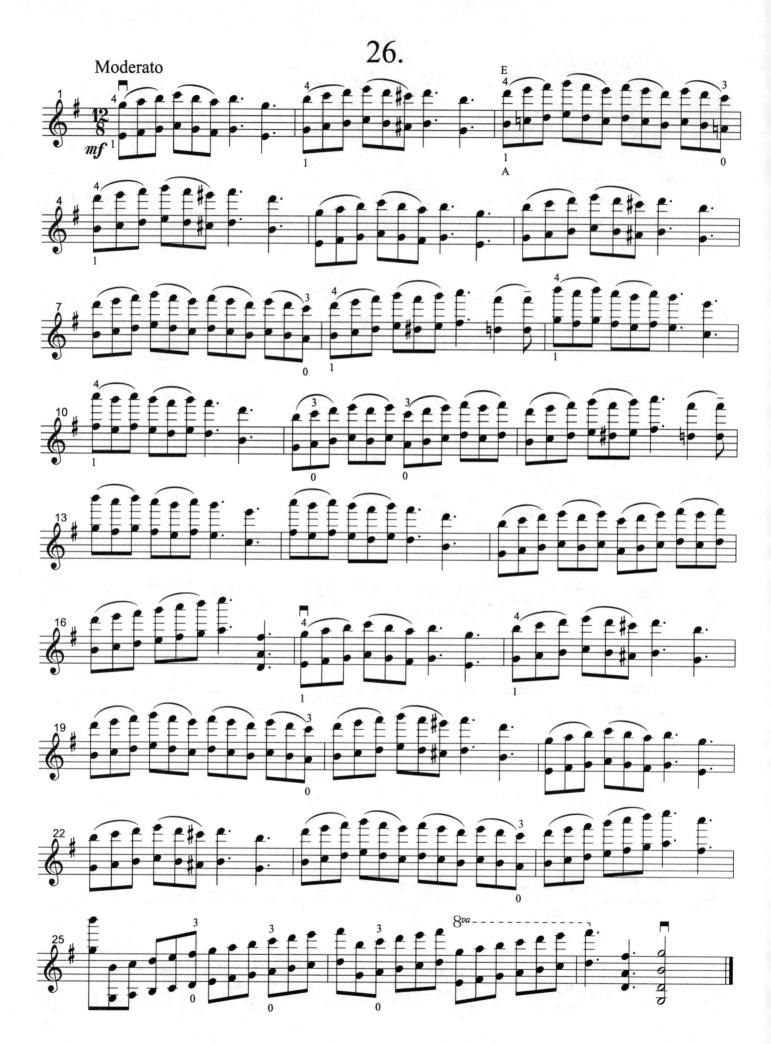

27.

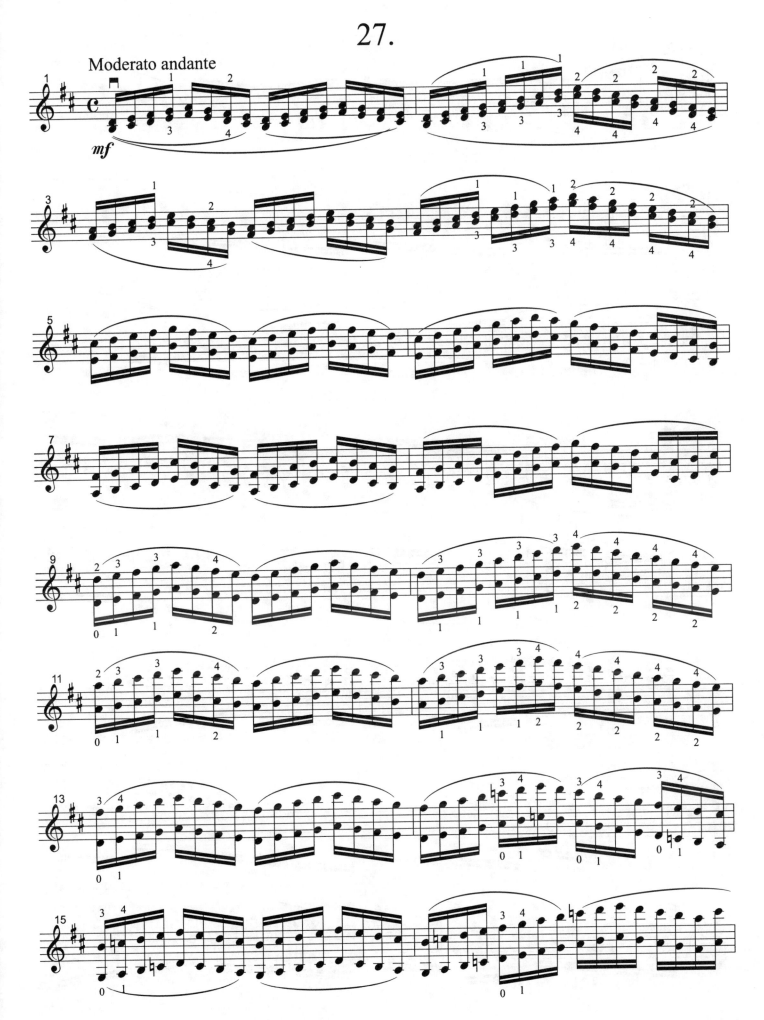

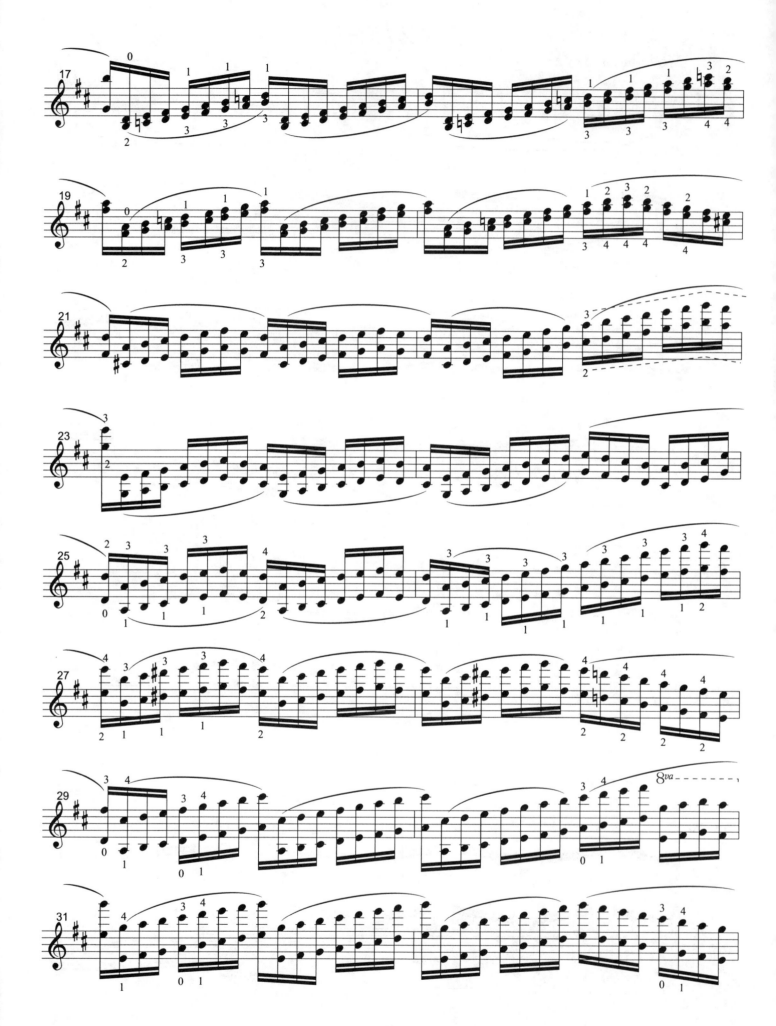

28.

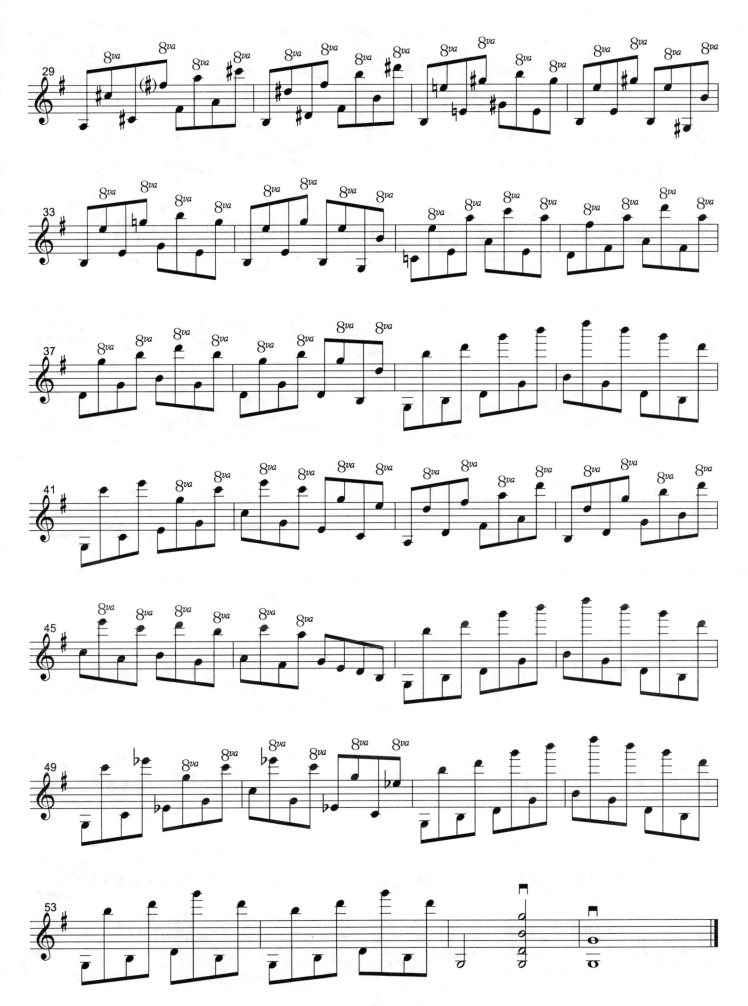

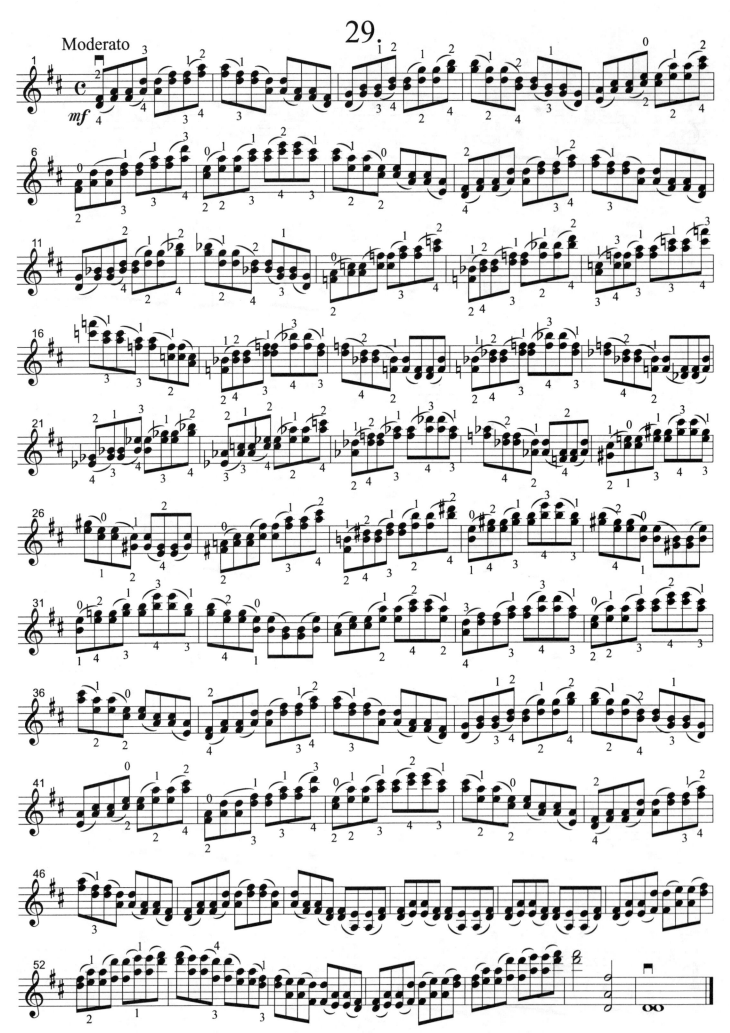

29.

Moderato

30.

31.

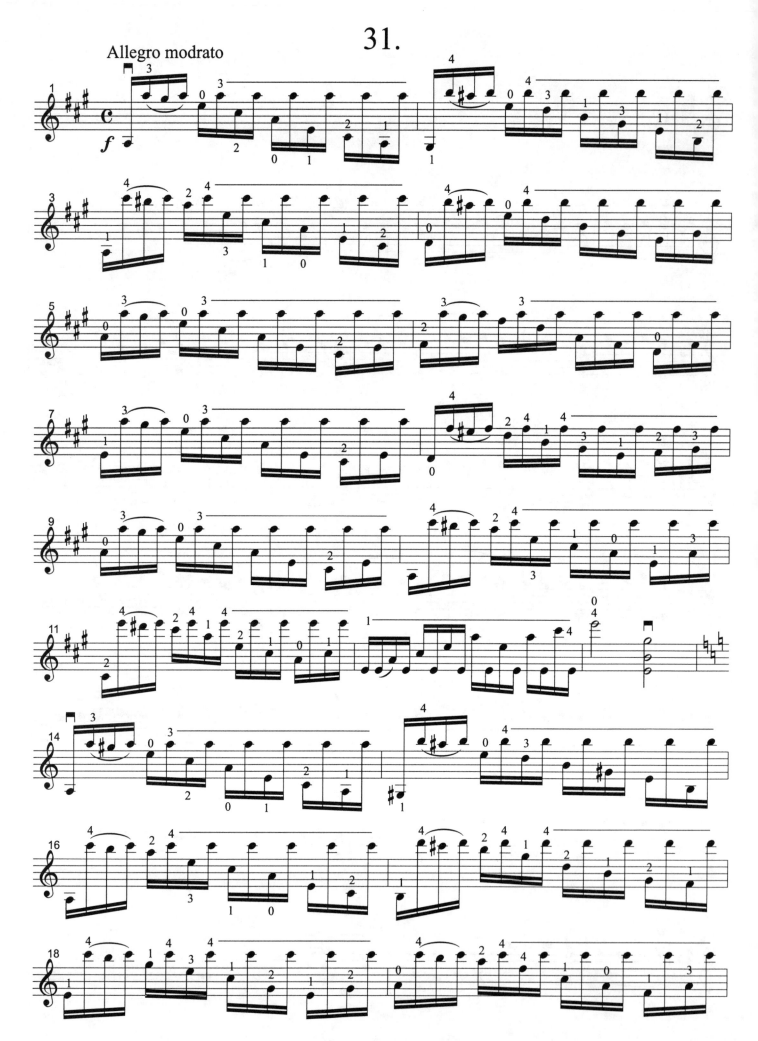

32.

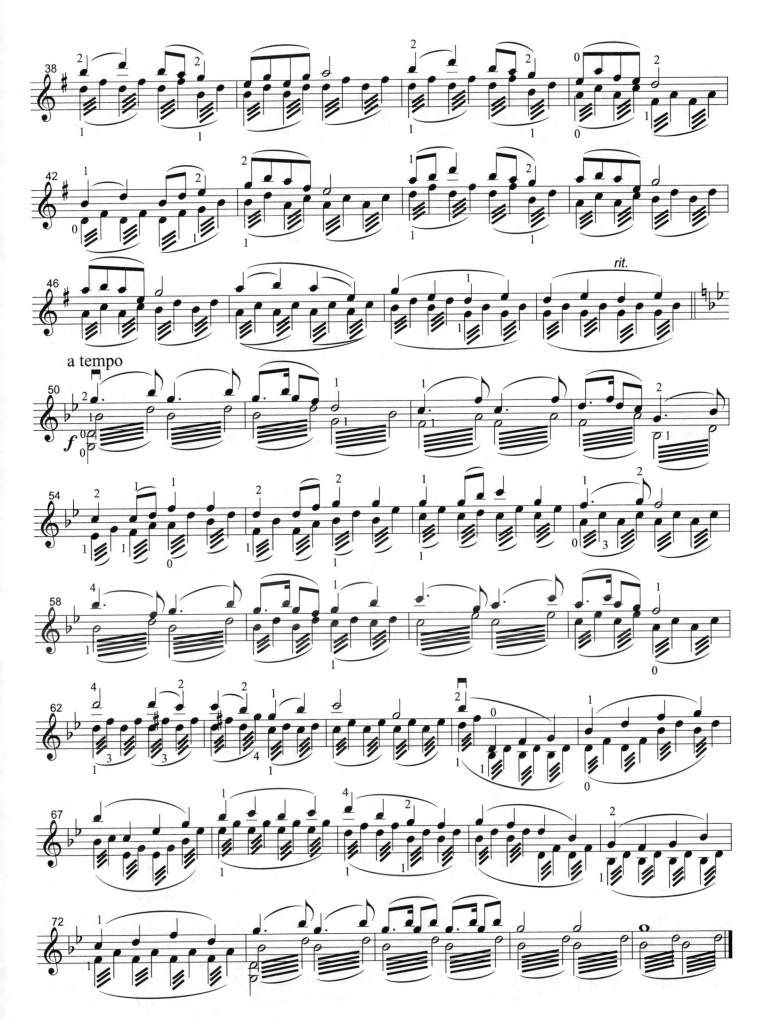

33.

34.

35.

36.

Preparatory exercises for Study No. 36

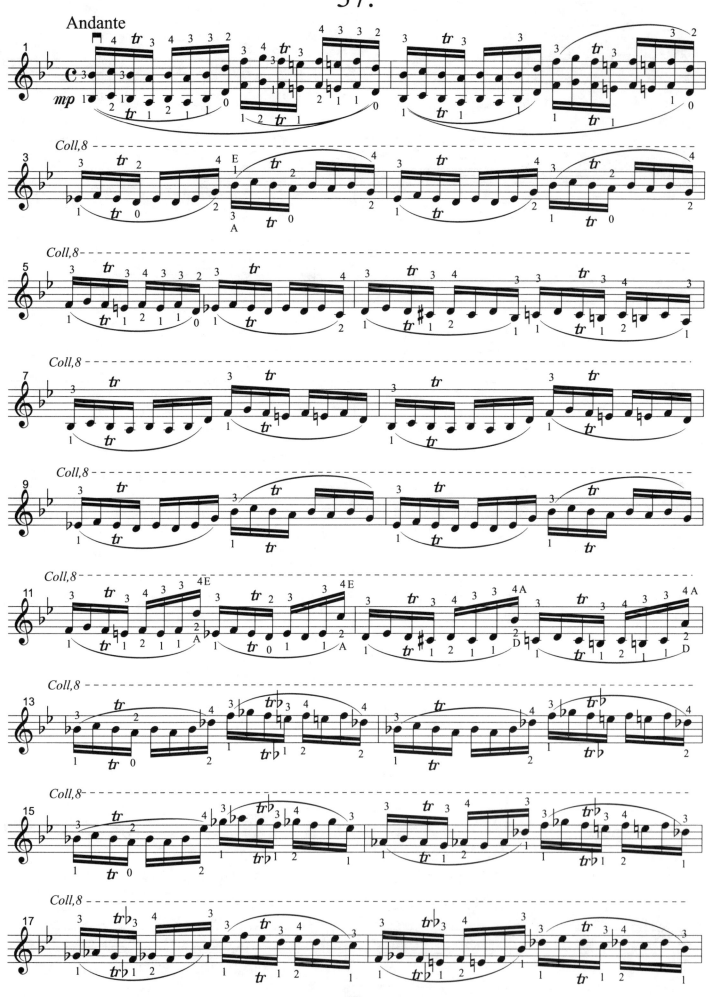

38.

39.

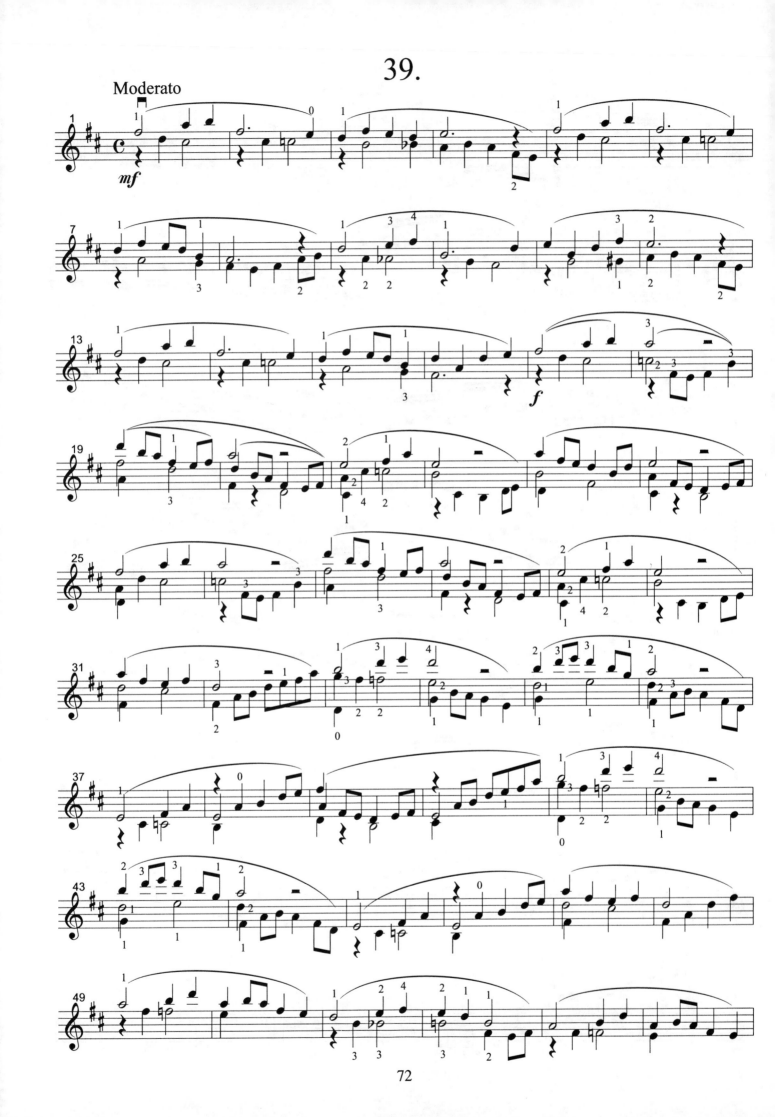